this book belongs to:

_____

twirl

written and illustrated by
Emily Lex

HARVEST
Kids

HARVEST HOUSE PUBLISHERS
EUGENE, OREGON

for my audrey girl

The Scripture quotation of Zephaniah 3:17 is taken from the Holy Bible, New Living Translation, copyright © 1996, 2004, 2015 by Tyndale House Foundation. Used by permission of Tyndale House Publishers, Inc., Carol Stream, Illinois 60188. All rights reserved.

The Scripture quotation of 1 Thessalonians 5:16-18 is taken from the Holy Bible, New International Version®, NIV®. Copyright © 1973, 1978, 1984, 2011 by Biblica, Inc.® Used by permission. All rights reserved worldwide.

Cover design by Nicole Dougherty

Interior design by Left Coast Design

Hand lettering by Emily Lex

Published in association with Illuminate Literary Agency: www.illuminateliterary.com

Ⓜ is a federally registered trademark of the Hawkins Children's LLC. Harvest House Publishers, Inc., is the exclusive licensee of the trademark.

Twirl

Text and artwork copyright © 2021 by Emily Lex

Published by Harvest House Publishers

Eugene, Oregon 97408

www.harvesthousepublishers.com

ISBN 978-0-7369-8039-5 (hardcover)

Library of Congress Catalogue-in-Publication Control Number: 2020055666

Printed in China

21 22 23 24 25 26 27 28 29 / **LP** / 10 9 8 7 6 5 4 3 2 1

The Lord your God is living among you.

He is a mighty savior.

He will take delight in you with gladness.

With his love, he will calm all your fears.

He will rejoice over you with joyful songs.

Zephaniah 3:17

Audrey girl loved to twirl.

She twirled in the morning.
She twirled at night.

She twirled through piles
of crunchy leaves

and under the jolly glow
of twinkling lights.

Audrey twirled in
fresh rain puddles

and while eating double-decker
ice cream cones.

Day after day, a delightful feeling bubbled up inside her.

It
sParkled

and
flowed
through her fingers
and toes

as she spun and leaped and danced so freely and lightly.

Yes, Audrey girl loved to twirl.

One afternoon, Audrey put on her favorite
twirling dress and her favorite twirling shoes
and went to the meadow beyond her house,

where the birds sang their songs
and the honeybees hummed
and the wildflowers blew in the breeze.

As she skipped along, she came upon a duck

swirling

whirling

dipping

and
bobbing
in a pond.

Oooh, what lovely twirling!

"Mr. Duck," Audrey said,
"can you show me how
to twirl like you?"

"Of course," replied Mr. Duck.
"Simply paddle your feet and throw back
your feathers and let the water move you."

Audrey dipped her toes in the water,
tossed her arms back…

…and slipped on the pebbles with a splash!

She didn't have feathers like Mr. Duck
and didn't float like Mr. Duck.
And even though she tried,
she just couldn't twirl like Mr. Duck.

She picked herself up, and on she went
as the birds sang their songs
and the honeybees hummed
and the wildflowers blew in the breeze.

She came upon a butterfly

flitting

flapping

and
gliding
gracefully through the air.

Oooh, what lovely twirling!

"Miss Butterfly," Audrey said,
"can you show me how
to twirl like you?"

"Of course," replied Miss Butterfly.
"Simply flap your wings and close your eyes
and let the wind carry you."

With eyes squeezed shut,
Audrey stretched tall on
her highest tippy toes,
fluttered her arms...

...and toppled to the ground—kerplop!

She didn't have wings like Miss Butterfly
and couldn't fly like Miss Butterfly.
And even though she tried, she just
couldn't twirl like Miss Butterfly.

She took a deep breath, and on she went
as the birds sang their songs
and the honeybees hummed
and the wildflowers blew in the breeze.

A bunny hopped by,

sPringing

flipping

and tumbling
through the wildflowers.

Oooh, what lovely twirling!

"Little Bunny," Audrey said,
"can you show me how to twirl like you?"

"Of course," replied Little Bunny.
"Simply wiggle your tail and hop up high
and let the ground lift you."

Audrey wiggled and bounced
and cartwheeled through the daisies...

...and landed in a dizzy heap.

She didn't have springy legs like Little Bunny
and couldn't flip like Little Bunny. And even though
she tried, she just couldn't twirl like Little Bunny.

Audrey brushed herself off
and rested beneath a tree.

Suddenly she didn't feel so free.

A hush came over the meadow.
Mr. Duck, Miss Butterfly, and Little Bunny
gathered around their friend.

"Audrey girl, you love to twirl!
Why have you stopped twirling?"

"Maybe twirling is not for me," she replied with a sigh.
"I can't float like Mr. Duck, and I can't fly like
Miss Butterfly, and I can't hop like Little Bunny.
Maybe I'm not made to twirl."

"But don't you see?" they said brightly.

"Your
loop-de-loop
leaps

and
tippy-toed
turns

are perfectly and wonderfully made!

God loves you and created you with your own
special twirl. You are exactly as He wants you to be."

A delightful feeling began
to bubble inside her.

It
glittered

and
glowed

from her head to her toes until she couldn't sit still any longer.

She rose to her feet, stretched her arms wide, and tilted
her face to the sky, letting the sun shine over her.

The birds sang their songs
and the honeybees hummed
and the wildflowers blew in the breeze.

And Audrey and her friends
twirled with all their hearts,
each in their own lovely way.

ABOUT THE AUTHOR

Emily Lex wrote all the words and painted all the pictures you see in this book.

When Emily was young, she dreamed of being a mom, an artist, a teacher, and a morning talk-show host. It turns out that she did become a mom, an artist, and a teacher (she teaches others how to paint).

While Emily's morning talk show hasn't happened yet, she is grateful that God has allowed her to become exactly who He made her to be.

Emily found her own special "twirl," and so can you!

EMILY'S FAVORITES

flower	color	snack	animal	hobby

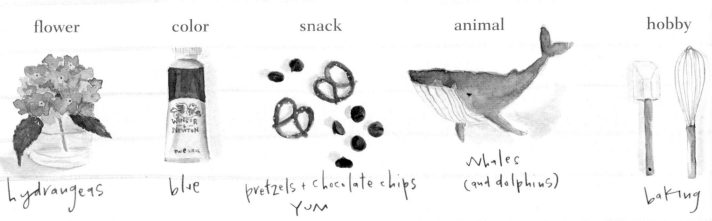

hydrangeas   blue   pretzels + chocolate chips
Yum   Whales (and dolphins)   baking